P9-BXX-374

ALISTAIR UNDERWATER

by Marilyn Sadler
Illustrated by Roger Bollen

Simon and Schuster Books for Young Readers
Published by Simon & Schuster Inc., New York

Alistair Grittle lived the quiet life of an ordinary schoolboy.

Every morning at dawn he had·a breakfast of oatmeal
without any sugar.

He brushed his teeth and his hair, as well as his jacket.

Then he went to school and reminded his teacher to collect
the homework.

In the evenings, Alistair worked with his chemistry set in the basement. His parents never heard a sound from him, unless, of course, there was an explosion.

But on weekends Alistair did what he loved best.

He collected duckweed and algae from the small pond
behind his house.

Almost everything that lived in Alistair's pond lived in his room as well.

He wished he could spend as much time at the bottom of his pond as he did at the top. But without gills, that was quite impossible.

So one day Alistair built himself a submarine.

One day Alistair was circling the bottom of his pond when he noticed a small opening in its floor. He was quite concerned that he might be missing some pond life.

So he put his submarine into gear and headed down
through the tunnel.

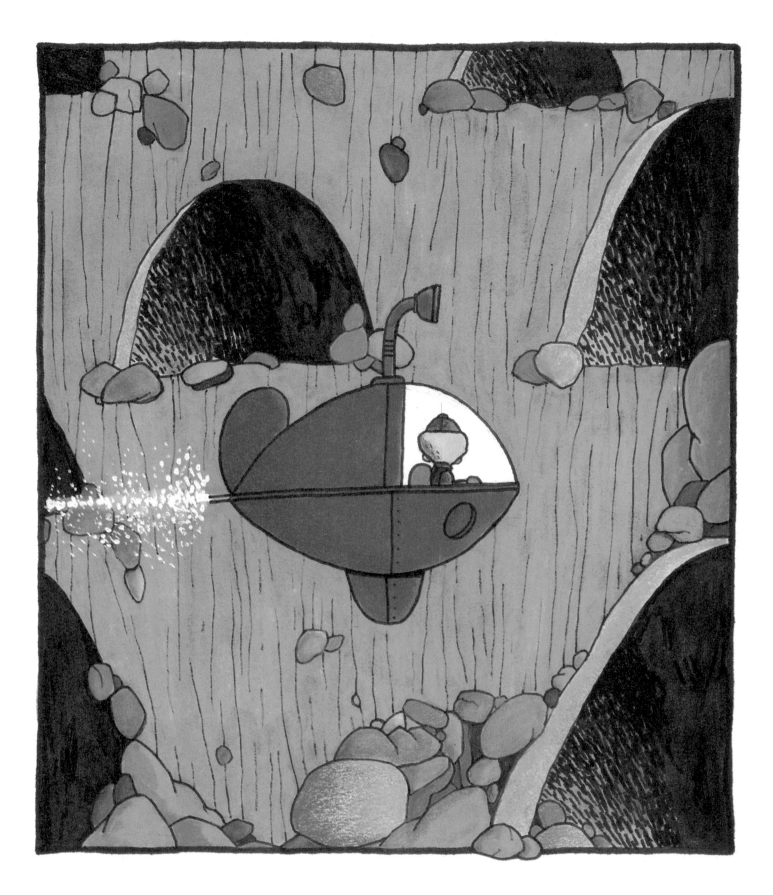

Alistair soon realized that there was more than one tunnel under his pond. In fact there were hundreds of tunnels going off in all directions.

Every turn he took led him deeper into the earth. He saw creatures he did not recognize from his own pond.

Then all of a sudden, Alistair's tunnel emptied out into an enormous underground cavern.

Alistair parked his submarine by the side of a rock and got out to take a water sample. He was about to unstop his test-tube when he thought he heard a noise.

Alistair turned around just in time to see some frog people disappear behind a rock.

When the frog people realized that Alistair was not going to hurt them, they came back out to meet him. Alistair liked the frog people. They reminded him of the frogs back in his own pond.

The frog people invited Alistair to have lunch with them.
Although Alistair liked the salad, he didn't touch the flies.

After lunch, the frog babies wanted to sit in Alistair's submarine. Alistair made them promise not to touch anything.

One of the frog babies was just about to touch the controls when all of a sudden something quite large and powerful came rushing through the water.

Alistair and the frog babies were sent flying through the air.

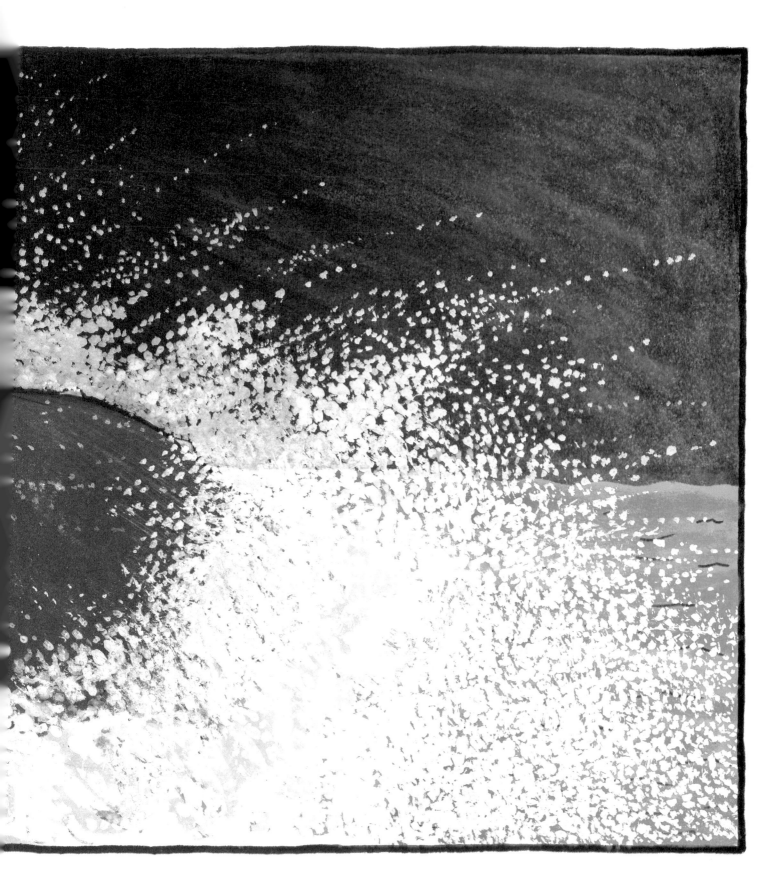

Alistair wanted to help the frog people, but he did not know what to do. Then he had an idea.

He got into his submarine and started up the engine. The frog people watched nervously from behind the rocks.

Alistair waited until he saw the Gooze coming. Then he took off in his submarine toward the tunnels.

The Gooze followed Alistair, just as he had hoped.

Alistair raced through the tunnels with the Gooze close behind him.

After many quick turns and clever moves, Alistair was certain he had lost the Gooze.

The frog people were so happy they croaked for joy. It was the first time they'd been able to swim in the stream for a very long time. And it was the first time the frog babies had been swimming at all.

Everyone wanted Alistair to stay for supper. But Alistair was anxious to get back to his own pond, so he said goodbye.

Alistair thought about the frog people all the way home. He was so pleased that he had been able to help them.

Now he could go back to his quiet life as an ordinary
school boy, knowing that the Gooze would never again . . .

. . . bother anyone.

MMAUS PUBLIC LIBRARY
MMAUS, PA 18049